THE MYSTERIOUS ADVENTURE

UNRAVEILING SECRETS

K.ROOPTHY KALADHAR

This book is lovingly dedicated to my dear friends,

Sreeja, Namratha, Susmitha, Dharani, Anjali, Akash, Peter, Jennie, and Ram,

Your unwavering support, encouragement, and friendship have meant the world to me. Through laughter and tears, you have been my constant companions, and I am forever grateful.

May the stories within these pages touch your hearts and remind you of the power of love, friendship, and the unbreakable bonds that unite us.

With love and appreciation,
K.Roopthy kaladhar.

Contents

Contents

Preface

In the quiet city of willow brook, a group of high school students find themselves drawn together by fate. Ria, Advik, Dev, Ava, Hazel, and Marcus may seem like ordinary teenagers, but their lives are about to take a thrilling turn.

Join them as they navigate the challenges of school, friendship, and family, all while uncovering the secrets of a mysterious haunted house. As they delve deeper into its dark corridors and hidden chambers, they will face perilous trials, unearth long-buried secrets, and confront malevolent forces that seek to consume them.

But amidst the darkness, there is also light. Love blossoms, friendships are forged, and courage shines bright as they stand together against the terrors that lurk in the shadows. And as they journey through the haunted house, they will discover that the greatest mysteries of all lie within themselves.

Prepare to embark on an unforgettable adventure filled with suspense, thrills, and unexpected twists. For in the world of the haunted house, nothing is as it seems, and every turn of the page brings new revelations and heart-pounding excitement.

Welcome to the world of "The Mysterious adventure" let us find out "the unveiling secrets".

Prologue

In the heart of the Willow Brook, nestled amidst the familiar sights and sounds of everyday life, looms a house that defies explanation. Its weathered facade stands as a silent testament to the passage of time, its windows like vacant eyes peering out into the world with a sense of foreboding.

For generations, the house has been a source of speculation and fear, its history steeped in legend and myth. Some say it was once the grand estate of a nobleman fallen from grace, its halls haunted by the echoes of his misdeeds. Others whisper of a darker past, claiming the land was once a sacred burial ground disturbed by the hand of man.

But for six high school students— Ria , Advik, Dev, Ava, Hazel, and Marcus—the house is more than just a tale to be told around a campfire. It's a challenge, a dare exchanged among friends on a lazy summer afternoon—a chance to test their bravery and prove their mettle in the face of the unknown.

Ria: The spirited leader of the group, Ria's courage knows no bounds. With a heart as big as her imagination, she leads her friends fearlessly into the unknown, determined to uncover the truth hidden within the house's darkened halls.

Advik: The steadfast protector, Advik's unwavering bravery is matched only by his loyalty to his friends. With a strong arm and a quick wit, he stands ready to defend his companions against whatever dangers they may encounter.

Dev: The quiet strength of the group, Dev's steady presence provides a sense of stability in the face of uncertainty. With a calm demeanor and a keen eye for detail, he navigates the challenges they face with unwavering determination.

Ava: The curious adventurer, Ava's thirst for knowledge often leads her into trouble. With a love for the mysterious and the unknown, she is always the first to delve into the secrets that lie hidden within the house's walls.

Hazel: The introspective thinker, Hazel's analytical mind is a valuable asset to the group. With a knack for solving puzzles and unraveling mysteries, she helps guide her friends through the labyrinthine corridors of the haunted house.

Marcus: The cautious skeptic, Marcus reluctance to believe in the supernatural often puts him at odds with his more adventurous friends. But beneath his skepticism lies a deep loyalty and a fierce determination to protect those he cares about.

Together, they stand on the threshold of an adventure unlike any they've ever known. As they step through the doors of the haunted house, they will confront fears they never knew they had, uncover secrets long buried in the shadows, and ultimately discover the true meaning of friendship, courage, and sacrifice.

But whether they emerge from their ordeal unscathed or fall prey to the darkness that lurks within remains to be seen. For in the world of the haunted house, nothing is as it seems, and danger lurks around every corner. The adventure begins now...

CHAPTER I

Detention Room Discovery

Marcas: (panting) Ria, we're late again. Hurry up!

Ria: (rushing out) I'm coming! Let's go, Marcas.

Marcas: (grumbling) Why does this always happen to us?

Ria: (trying to lighten the mood) Well, at least we're in this together, right?

(Ria and Marcas arrive at school and end up in detention with their friends.)

Advik: (jokingly) So, Marcas, what's the plan for today? How are we going to get out of this one?

Dev: (chiming in) We're in this mess because of you three. Mixing chemicals in class? Really?

Ava: (excitedly) Hey, at least we're all together. Detention buddies!

(Hazel enters the room with a somber expression.)

Ria: (surprised) Hazel, you're here too? What happened?

Hazel: (sadly) I got detention for helping Prisha with her assignment. Professor Marcus wasn't happy about it.

(Principal enters and assigns them the task of cleaning a restricted storeroom.)

Marcas: (concerned) Sir, isn't that room off-limits?

Principal: (authoritatively) Just do as I say.

(As they clean, Ria discovers a mysterious map.)

Ria: Guys, look at this! It's a map to a house, six kilometers away from here. And there's a strange message at the bottom.

אם אתה רוצה למצוא את הקופסה, עקוב אחר המקום שבו השמיים פוגשים"
את האור, היא מראה השתקפות בחושך

(The message reads: "If you want to find the box, follow where the sky meets the light, it shows reflection in the dark.").

CHAPTER II

The Mysterious House

Ria: (examining the map) This is intriguing. What do you think it means?

Hazel: (curiously) Maybe it's a clue to some hidden treasure or a secret place.

Dev: (skeptically) Treasure hunt? Sounds like something out of a movie.

Ava: (excitedly) Come on, guys! Let's check it out. It'll be fun!

Advik: (adventurously) I'm in. Who knows what we might find?

Marcas: (nervously) Are we really going to do this? It sounds risky.

Ria: (determined) We'll stick together. It'll be an adventure.

(The group decides to follow the map and head towards the mysterious house. As they walk, they discuss their theories about the message.)

Dev: (analyzing) "Where the sky meets the light, it shows reflection in the dark." What could that mean?

Hazel: (thinking) Maybe it's referring to a place where the sun sets, and its reflection can be seen in the darkness.

Ava: (excitedly) That's possible! Like a lake or a pond where the water reflects the sky.

(After walking for a while, they arrive at the creepy-looking house mentioned in the map.)

Advik: (looking at the house) This place gives me the chills. Are we sure about this?

Ria: (encouragingly) We've come this far. Let's see what's inside.

(They cautiously enter the house, their hearts pounding with anticipation. The inside is dark and musty, filled with cobwebs and dust.)

Marcas: (whispering) It feels like we're in a horror movie.

Hazel: (shivering) I hope there are no ghosts here.

Dev: (trying to lighten the mood) Don't worry, Hazel. I'll protect you.

(As they explore further, they stumble upon a hidden room at the end of a corridor. It's locked with a rusty padlock.)

Ava: (excitedly) Look! That must be where the box is hidden.

Ria: (determined) Let's find a way to open it.

(They search the room and discover a key hidden under an old rug. With bated breath, they unlock the padlock and open the door.)

CHAPTER III

The Hidden Chamber

(As the door creaks open, the group is met with darkness. They cautiously step inside, their senses alert.)

Advik: (whispering) It's so dark in here. Does anyone have a flashlight?

Hazel: (rummaging through her bag) I have one.

(Ria switches on the flashlight, illuminating the room. What they see takes their breath away.)

Dev: (in awe) Whoa, look at this!

(The room is filled with ancient artifacts, mysterious symbols etched into the walls, and an ornate chest in the center.)

Ava: (excitedly) This is amazing! It's like something out of a history book.

Marcas: (examining the symbols) These symbols look familiar. I think I've seen them before.

Ria: (examining the chest) Let's see what's inside.

(She cautiously opens the chest, revealing a collection of old scrolls and trinkets.)

Hazel: (examining the scrolls) These must hold some valuable information.

Advik: (picking up a trinket) And these trinkets seem ancient. They must have some significance.

Dev: (curiously) I wonder who lived here and why they hid all this away.

(The group starts examining the scrolls and trinkets, trying to decipher their meaning.)

Ria: (excitedly) Look at this scroll. It seems to be a map of the city, but with markings we've never seen before.

Hazel: (studying the trinkets) And these symbols on the trinkets, they match the ones on the walls.

Ava: (realizing) What if this is a clue to something bigger? Something hidden within the city?

(The group's curiosity is piqued as they delve deeper into the mysteries of the hidden chamber.)

CHAPTER IV

Unraveling the Mystery

(Ria carefully unrolls the scroll, revealing intricate markings and symbols.)

Ria: (examining the scroll) These symbols... they seem to correspond to specific locations in the city.

Hazel: (pointing at the map) Look here. This symbol matches the one on the trinkets we found.

Dev: (excitedly) So, if we follow these symbols on the map, we might uncover more clues.

(The group decides to follow the symbols on the map, embarking on a journey across the city.)

Advik: (as they walk) This feels like we're part of a real-life treasure hunt.

Marcas: (nervously) I hope we're not getting in over our heads.

Ria: (encouragingly) We'll be fine, Marcas. We're in this together.

(As they follow the map, they encounter various challenges and obstacles.)

Ava: (pointing ahead) Look, that symbol matches the one on the map.

Hazel: (excitedly) Let's see what's there.

(They arrive at a dilapidated building, its walls covered in ivy and graffiti.)

Dev: (examining the building) This must be one of the locations marked on the map.

Ria: (determined) Let's go inside and see what we can find.

(Inside the building, they discover a hidden chamber similar to the one they found in the mysterious house.)

Hazel: (in awe) It's like we're uncovering a hidden world within our city.

Advik: (examining the artifacts) These must hold some important significance.

(Suddenly, they hear footsteps approaching.)

Marcas: (whispering) Someone's coming. We need to hide.

(The group hides as a figure enters the chamber. It's Professor Marcus, their teacher.)

Professor Marcus: (surprised) What are you all doing here?

Ria: (nervously) We... we were just exploring.

Professor Marcus: (examining the artifacts) These are ancient relics. How did you find them?

(The group explains everything to Professor Marcus, who listens intently.)

Professor Marcus: (impressed) You've stumbled upon something remarkable. These artifacts hold the key to unlocking a centuries-old mystery.

(The group realizes that their adventure is far from over as they prepare to delve deeper into the secrets of their city.)

CHAPTER V

Echoes of the Past

(Marcas cautiously reaches for the ornate chest in the hidden chamber of the haunted house. With trembling hands, he slowly lifts the lid, revealing an array of ancient artifacts. Among them, he notices a small telescope, its brass fmarcase glinting in the dim light.)

Marcas: (intrigued) What's this doing here?

(As he reaches out to touch the telescope, a strange sensation washes over him. It's as if the air around him has grown heavier, charged with an unseen energy. Before he can investigate further, he hears Ava's voice calling out to him from outside.)

Ava: (calling) Marcas! Are you there? We should leave before it gets too late.

(Marcas hesitates, torn between the curiosity of exploring the telescope and the urgency of Ava's call. Reluctantly, he places the telescope back into the chest and closes the lid.)

Marcas: (to himself) I'll come back for you later.

(As he turns to leave, a faint whisper echoes in his ears. At first, he dismisses it as his imagination playing tricks on him. But as he takes a few steps towards the exit, the whispers grow louder, more insistent.)

Voice: (whispering) Marcas... Marcas...

(Marcas freezes, his heart pounding in his chest. He looks around, searching for the source of the voice, but there's no one else in the chamber.)

Marcas: (uneasy) Who's there? Show yourself!

(The whispers continue, echoing off the walls of the chamber, filling the air with an eerie intensity. Marcas's breath quickens as he struggles to make sense of what's happening.)

Marcas: (panicked) This isn't real. It can't be real.

(With a sense of foreboding weighing heavily on his shoulders, Marcas rushes out of the chamber, eager to rejoin his friends. But the whispers continue to haunt him, lingering in the recesses of his mind like ghosts of the past.)

CHAPTER VI

Shadows of the Past

(Marcas emerges from the hidden chamber, his mind still reeling from the unsettling whispers that had enveloped him moments ago. Outside, the air feels heavy, as if the atmosphere itself is holding its breath.)

Marcas: (to himself) Get a grip, Marcas. It was just your imagination.

(He tries to shake off the feeling of unease as he rejoins his friends who are waiting anxiously outside.)

Ava: (concerned) Are you okay, Marcas? You look pale.

Marcas: (forcing a smile) Yeah, I'm fine. Just a little spooked, that's all.

Ria: (noticing his unease) Did you find anything inside?

Marcas: (hesitantly) Just some old artifacts. Nothing too exciting.

(As they make their way out of the haunted house, Marcas can't shake the feeling of being watched. Every shadow seems to hold a secret, every whisper a hidden message.)

Hazel: (noticing his distraction) Marcas, are you sure you're okay?

Marcas: (forcing himself to focus) Yeah, I'm fine. Let's just get out of here.

(They hurry away from the haunted house, the echoes of their footsteps mingling with the whispers that still linger in Marcas's mind.)

Dev: (noticing Marcas's unease) What's wrong with you, man? You've been acting strange ever since we left the chamber.

Marcas: (hesitantly) I... I heard something in there. Whispers, like someone calling my name.

Advik: (skeptically) You're probably just spooked from being in that creepy old house.

Marcas: (insistently) No, it felt real. Like there was someone else in there with me.

(The group exchanges concerned glances as they continue on their way. The shadows grow longer, casting a veil of darkness over the city.)

Ria: (gently) Maybe we should go back and investigate further. See if there's any truth to what Marcas heard.

Hazel: (nervously) I don't know... That place gave me the creeps.

Ava: (determined) We can't let fear hold us back. If there's something in that house, we need to find out what it is.

(With a newfound determination, the group sets off towards the haunted house once again, unaware of the secrets that lie hidden within its walls.)

CHAPTER VII

Whispers in the Dark

(As the group approaches the haunted house once again, a sense of foreboding hangs in the air. The whispers that had haunted Marcas inside the chamber seem to echo in the darkness, growing louder with each step.)

Advik: (whispering) Do you hear that?

Ria: (nervously) It sounds like... whispers.

(The group exchanges uneasy glances as they cautiously enter the house, their footsteps echoing in the eerie silence.)

Dev: (holding a flashlight) Let's stick together. We don't know what we might find in here.

(As they explore the dimly lit corridors, the whispers grow louder, swirling around them like a sinister melody.)

Ava: (shivering) This place gives me the creeps.

Hazel: (gripping her friend's arm) I don't like this, guys. I think we should leave.

(Marcas's heart races as he recalls the whispers he heard earlier. He can't shake the feeling that they're leading him somewhere, beckoning him towards a hidden truth.)

Marcas: (determined) No, we have to keep going. There's something in here we need to find.

(Advik and Ria exchange a worried glance, but they trust in Marcas's intuition. Together, they press on, following the whispers deeper into the heart of the house.)

Advik: (whispering) Do you think we're getting close to something?

Ria: (nodding) I can feel it. Whatever's in here, it's leading us somewhere.

(As they reach the chamber where Marcas had heard the whispers before, the air grows thick with anticipation. In the center of the room, they spot the ornate chest, its lid slightly ajar.)

Dev: (shining the flashlight) Look, the chest is open.

Marcas: (approaching cautiously) This is where I heard the whispers earlier.

(As he reaches out to investigate, the whispers suddenly stop, replaced by an eerie silence.)

Ava: (nervously) What's happening?

(A chill runs down their spines as they realize they're not alone in the chamber. Something—or someone—is watching them from the shadows.)

Hazel: (voice trembling) We need to get out of here. Now.

(But before they can make their escape, a figure emerges from the darkness, its eyes gleaming with malice.)

Figure: (sinisterly) You should not have come here. This place holds secrets that are not meant to be discovered.

(The group braces themselves for whatever lies ahead, knowing that they're about to confront the true depths of the haunted house's mysteries.)

CHAPTER VIII

Bonds of Love and Courage

(The figure steps forward menacingly, its presence casting a shadow over the group. Advik's instincts kick in as he steps in front of Ria, shielding her from the ominous figure.)

Advik: (firmly) Stay back! We won't let you harm us.

Figure: (sinisterly) You dare to defy me? You know nothing of the power that resides within these walls.

(Ria's heart races with fear as she clutches Advik's arm, her eyes wide with apprehension. But before the figure can make a move, Advik springs into action, his bravery shining through the darkness.)

Advik: (defiantly) We may not know everything, but we won't let fear control us. We're stronger together.

(With a swift and decisive motion, Advik confronts the figure, using his quick reflexes and resourcefulness to outmaneuver it. In a moment of bravery, he manages to disarm the figure, freeing the group from its grasp.)

Ria: (breathless) Advik, you saved us!

(A wave of relief washes over Ria as she gazes at Advik, her admiration and gratitude shining in her eyes. In that moment of vulnerability and gratitude, she finds herself drawn to him like never before.)

Ria: (softly) Are you okay?

(Advik meets Ria's gaze, his heart pounding with emotion. Without a word, he pulls her into a tight embrace, holding her close as if to shield her from any further harm.)

Advik: (whispering) I'm fine now, as long as you're safe.

(Ria feels a rush of warmth and affection as she buries her face in Advik's chest, her heart overflowing with love and gratitude for the brave and caring man who stands before her.)

(The group stands together, united by their shared courage and determination. As they leave the haunted house behind, they know that their bond has been strengthened by the trials they've faced together.)

Advik and Ria's embrace, a testament to the power of love and bravery in the face of darkness

CHAPTER IX

Veil of Shadows

(The figure, disarmed by Advik's bravery, retreats into the shadows, its presence lingering like a ghost in the haunted house. With a newfound sense of urgency, the group hurries to leave the eerie chamber behind, their hearts still racing from the encounter.)

Ria: (breathlessly) We need to get out of here before it comes back.

Advik: (nodding) Agreed. Let's go.

(The group rushes out of the haunted house, the echoes of their footsteps reverberating in the darkness. As they emerge into the cool night air, they realize that they are not alone. A shadowy figure lurks in the shadows, its eyes gleaming with malevolence.)

Ava: (pointing) Look! There it is again!

(The figure moves closer, its presence sending shivers down their spines. With nowhere to run, they brace themselves for another confrontation.)

Figure: (ominously) You cannot escape the darkness. It will consume you all.

(Marcas's mind races as he tries to make sense of the figure's cryptic words. What secrets lie hidden within the haunted house, and why is the figure so intent on guarding them?)

Marcas: (firmly) We won't let you stop us. We'll uncover the truth, no matter what it takes.

(The figure laughs mockingly, its laughter echoing in the night like a sinister symphony.)

Figure: (tauntingly) You think you can defy fate? You're just children playing at bravery. You have no idea what you're up against.

(The group stands their ground, their determination unshaken by the figure's threats. With a defiant glint in their eyes, they prepare to face whatever challenges lie ahead.)

Advik: (stepping forward) We may be young, but we're not afraid to fight for what's right. And we won't rest until we uncover the secrets of this place.

(The figure's laughter fades into the night as it retreats into the darkness, leaving the group to wonder what other dangers await them in the shadows.)

Ria: (gripping Advik's hand) We can't let fear hold us back. We have to keep going, no matter what.

(The group nods in agreement, their resolve strengthened by their shared courage and determination. With a sense of purpose driving them forward, they set out to uncover the truth behind the haunted house's mysteries.)

the group facing a new challenge, their resolve tested by the shadowy figure's ominous warnings. As they venture deeper into the unknown, they must steel themselves for whatever dangers lie ahead.

CHAPTER X

Shadows of Deception

(As the group delves deeper into the mysteries surrounding the haunted house, they remain wary of the shadowy figure that haunts their every step. However, unbeknownst to them, the true villain lurks in the most unexpected of places—their own school.)

Ria : (whispering) I can't shake the feeling that Marcus knows more than he's letting on.

Adivk: (nodding) It's strange how he seemed so interested in the artifacts we found. I wonder if he has a connection to this place.

(The group's suspicions about Professor Marcus continue to grow as they recall his peculiar behavior and cryptic remarks. But little do they know, the real mastermind behind the shadows is someone much closer to home—their own principal.)

Dev: (examining the artifacts) Marcus seems genuinely interested in this stuff. Maybe he's just a history buff.

Hazel: (doubtfully) I don't know, Dev. There's something about him that doesn't sit right with me.

(The group's suspicions reach a boiling point when they discover a hidden compartment in one of the artifacts, containing a note signed by their principal. The note contains cryptic instructions and hints at a deeper conspiracy.)

Ava: (reading the note) It says here that the artifacts are key to unlocking a great power—one that our principal seeks to control.

Marcas: (shocked) But why would he want to do that? What does he stand to gain?

(The group realizes that they've been deceived all along, their trust misplaced in the wrong person. As they confront the truth, they must band together to stop their principal from unleashing the ancient power hidden within the artifacts.)

Advik: (determined) We have to stop him before it's too late. We can't let him use the power of the artifacts for his own selfish desires.

Ria: (resolutely) Agreed. We'll need to use all of our skills and cunning to outsmart him and uncover the truth behind his sinister plans.

(With their determination renewed, the group sets out to confront their principal and put an end to his reign of deception. Little do they know, the true test of their courage and loyalty lies just ahead, as they face off against the darkness that lurks within their own school.)

the group preparing to confront their principal, unaware of the dangers that await them and the true extent of the conspiracy that threatens to consume them all. As they venture deeper into the heart of the mystery, they must rely on each other to uncover the truth and put an end to the darkness once and for all.

CHAPTER XI

Unveiling the Conspiracy

(Determined to uncover the truth behind their principal's sinister plans, the group embarks on a daring mission to confront him. With hearts pounding and adrenaline coursing through their veins, they navigate the labyrinthine corridors of their school, each step bringing them closer to the heart of the conspiracy.)

Ria: (whispering) We need to stay vigilant. Who knows what traps he may have set for us?

Advik: (nodding) Agreed. Let's keep our wits about us and watch each other's backs.

(The group moves stealthily through the shadows, their senses alert for any sign of danger. Suddenly, they hear voices up ahead—a sign that they're getting closer to their target.)

Hazel: (listening intently) I think I hear him talking. We must be close.

Dev: (gesturing) Let's go. We can't afford to waste any more time.

(As they round a corner, they come face to face with their principal, who stands before them with a sinister smile on his face.)

Principal: (smirking) Ah, so you've finally arrived. I've been expecting you.

(The group braces themselves for a confrontation, ready to expose the truth behind the principal's nefarious schemes.)

Ria: (firmly) We know what you're up to. You won't get away with this.

Principal: (laughing) Oh, but I already have. You see, you've played right into my hands.

(The principal reveals his true intentions, explaining how he manipulated them into uncovering the artifacts and bringing them to him.)

Advik: (shocked) But why? What do you hope to gain from all of this?

Principal: (smirking) Power, of course. With the artifacts under my control, I will have the ability to reshape the world in my image.

(The group realizes that they've been deceived from the very beginning, their trust in their principal misplaced. But as the principal prepares to unleash the ancient power of the artifacts, they refuse to back down.)

Marcas: (defiantly) We won't let you do this. We'll stop you, no matter what it takes.

(The group springs into action, using their skills and cunning to outsmart the principal and thwart his plans. With a combination of bravery, teamwork, and quick thinking, they manage to disable the artifacts and prevent the principal from achieving his dark ambitions.)

Ria: (panting) We did it. We stopped him.

Advik: (grinning) And we couldn't have done it without each other.

(As they emerge victorious from their showdown with the principal, the group realizes that their bond has been strengthened by the challenges they've faced together. With the truth finally revealed, they can rest easy knowing that they've saved their school—and perhaps the world—from the clutches of darkness.)

the group basking in their triumph, their spirits lifted by the knowledge that they've overcome the greatest challenge of their lives. As they prepare to return to their normal lives, they do so with a newfound sense of confidence and unity, ready to face whatever adventures lie ahead.

23

CHAPTER XII

Whispers Resurfaced

(After their previous victory, the group resumes their normal routines, hoping the whispers were just a distant memory. But soon, those eerie murmurs return, unsettling them once more.)

Ria: (anxiously) Did you hear that?

Advik: (listening closely) It's those whispers again.

(The group exchanges worried glances, realizing the threat they thought they'd defeated may still linger.)

Hazel: (nervously) How can this be happening? We stopped the principal, right?

Dev: (thoughtfully) Maybe there's someone else behind all of this.

(Their suspicions deepen when they receive a mysterious message, hinting at a resurgence of darkness.)

Ava: (reading the message) "The darkness will rise again."

Marcas: (determined) We can't let this happen. We have to find out who's behind it.

(The group embarks on a new quest, searching for answers beneath their school. In a hidden chamber, they find artifacts similar to before, but with an ominous aura.)

Ria: (examining the artifacts) These look like the ones we found earlier, but there's something different about them.

Advik: (scrutinizing the symbols) It's like they're trying to tell us something important.

(Suddenly, a sinister figure emerges, its presence filling the chamber with dread.)

Figure: (menacingly) You thought you could stop me. But you've only delayed the inevitable.

(The group prepares to face the darkness anew, knowing they must confront this threat head-on.)

the group ready to fight against the returning darkness, their determination unyielding despite the challenges ahead.

The Family Connection

(As the group dig deeper into the mystery, they stumble upon a revelation that shakes them to their core. Prisha, the seemingly ordinary classmate, holds a pivotal connection to the principal—an unexpected family tie that binds them to the heart of the enigma.)

Ria: (eyes widening in disbelief) Prisha... related to the principal? That's... unexpected.

Advik: (voice tinged with concern) It changes everything. But how does she fit into all of this?

(The group ponders over the implications of this newfound connection, their minds racing with questions about Prisha's role in the unfolding mystery.)

Hazel: (furrowing her brows) Prisha never mentioned anything about her family. Could they be involved in the secrets of the house?

Dev: (voice laced with suspicion) It wouldn't surprise me. There's something about her silence that doesn't sit right with me.

(The group's suspicions are heightened when they stumble upon a hidden diary belonging to Prisha's father—a diary that holds clues to the dark secrets lurking within the haunted house.)

Ava: (perusing the diary) "The artifacts hold immense power, but they must never be wielded by the wrong hands."

Marcas: (eyes widening in realization) Prisha's father knew about the dangers. But why didn't he intervene?

(The group comes to the unsettling realization that Prisha's family may hold the key to unraveling the mystery of the artifacts and the principal's intentions.)

Ria: (determined) We need to find Prisha. Perhaps she holds the missing pieces to this puzzle.

(The group sets out in search of Prisha, their minds buzzing with anticipation and trepidation. Little do they know, their quest for answers will lead them to confront the darkness that lurks within the haunted house—and to a confrontation with the principal that will test their resolve and unity.)

the group on the cusp of a pivotal encounter, as they prepare to confront Prisha and unravel the secrets that bind her family to the ominous forces that threaten their school and their very lives.

CHAPTER XIII

Unraveling the Enigma

(With the revelation of Prisha's familial ties to the principal, the group's quest for answers intensifies. Each step forward brings them closer to the heart of the mystery, shrouded in uncertainty and danger.)

Ria: (resolute) We have to find Prisha. She might hold the key to understanding everything.

Advik: (nodding) But let's tread carefully. We don't know what secrets she's keeping—or what dangers lie ahead.

(The group embarks on their search, navigating the labyrinthine corridors of the school with caution. Their senses are on high alert, every shadow holding the promise of revelation or peril.)

Hazel: (whispering) Prisha could be anywhere. We have to keep our eyes open.

Dev: (determined) We'll find her. And we'll uncover the truth, no matter what.

(After what feels like an eternity, they finally locate Prisha in the dimly lit library, her presence surrounded by an air of mystery.)

Hazel: (approaching cautiously) Prisha, we need to talk to you. It's urgent.

Prisha: (startled) What's going on? Why are you all here?

Dev: (gently) We know about your family's connection to the principal. Please, help us understand.

Prisha: (guarded) I... I can't. You don't understand the danger you're in.

(The group's suspicions deepen as Prisha's cryptic words hang in the air, but their conversation is interrupted by a chilling presence—a figure emerging from the shadows, its identity veiled in mystery.)

Figure: (sinisterly) So, you seek answers. But beware, the truth may lead you down a path from which there is no return.

(The group braces themselves for another confrontation, the tension thickening with each passing moment. Meanwhile, amidst the uncertainty and danger, a subtle spark of affection ignites between Dev and Hazel, their shared bond strengthening amidst the chaos.)

the group poised on the edge of discovery, their quest for truth entwined with danger and intrigue. As they prepare to confront the enigmatic figure and uncover the secrets hidden within the shadows, they know that their journey is far from over—and that the mysteries they unravel may forever change their lives

Into the Unknown

As the group confronts Prisha and the mysterious figure lurking in the shadows, they brace themselves for the unknown dangers that lie ahead. With each heartbeat, their resolve strengthens, but so does the sense of trepidation that fills the air.

Ria: "Prisha, please. We need to understand. Tell us what you know."

Prisha: "I can't... it's too dangerous."

Dev: "We're already in danger. Whatever it is, we can face it together."

Prisha's eyes flicker with uncertainty, torn between revealing the truth and protecting her friends. But before she can respond, the ominous figure steps forward, its presence sending a shiver down their spines.

Figure: "You fools. You think you can uncover the truth? You know nothing of the darkness that lurks within these walls."

With a swift motion, the figure summons shadows that envelop the room, trapping the group in a sinister embrace. Panic sets in as they struggle to break free, their hearts racing with fear.

Advik: "We have to get out of here. Now!"

But escape proves elusive as the shadows close in, threatening to swallow them whole. With each passing moment, their hopes dim, until suddenly, a glimmer of light breaks through the darkness—a faint echo of hope in the midst of despair.

Hazel: "Look! There's a way out!"

With renewed determination, they rally together, pushing back against the encroaching shadows with all their strength. Slowly but surely, they inch closer to freedom, their bonds of friendship and courage guiding them through the perilous darkness.

Just as they reach the brink of escape, a final obstacle looms before them—a towering figure blocking their path, its eyes gleaming with malice.

Figure: "You may have escaped for now, but remember this: the darkness will always find you."

With a chilling laugh, the figure vanishes into the shadows, leaving the group shaken but undeterred. As they emerge from the haunted depths of the school, they know that their journey is far from over—and that the greatest challenges still lie ahead.

the group facing their greatest peril yet, their bonds tested by the shadows that threaten to consume them. But amidst the darkness, a glimmer of hope remains, guiding them towards the light of a new dawn.

CHAPTER XIV

Shadows of the Past

The night hung heavy with an air of foreboding as the group ventured deeper into the heart of the mystery, their senses alert to the slightest whisper of danger. Around them, the darkness seemed to press in, its suffocating embrace threatening to swallow them whole.

Ria: (whispering) We need to find out more about Prisha's family. There must be clues somewhere.

Advik: (nodding) Agreed. But we have to be careful. We don't know what—or who—we might encounter in these shadows.

The group moved cautiously through the abandoned corridors of the school, their footsteps echoing in the eerie silence. Each shadow seemed to hold a secret, each whisper a warning of the perils that lay ahead.

Hazel: (shivering) I can't shake the feeling that we're being watched.

Dev: (tightening his grip on Hazel's hand) Don't worry. I've got you. We'll get through this together.

Their whispered reassurances were a beacon of light in the suffocating darkness, a reminder that even in the face of fear, love could still flourish.

As they delved deeper into the labyrinthine depths of the school, they stumbled upon a hidden chamber—a chamber filled with relics of a forgotten time, each one whispering secrets of the past.

Ava: (breathlessly) Look at this! It's like stepping into another world.

Marcas: (examining the artifacts) These must be centuries old. But why were they hidden away?

Their questions hung in the air unanswered, the mystery deepening with each passing moment. But as they ventured further into the chamber, they uncovered a clue—a clue that would lead them to the truth they sought.

Ria: (excitedly) Look! It's a journal. Maybe it belonged to Prisha's father.

With trembling hands, they opened the journal, its pages filled with cryptic writings and faded ink. As they read, a sense of dread washed over them, for they knew that the answers they sought were closer than they ever imagined.

But just as they were on the verge of uncovering the truth, a shadowy figure emerged from the darkness—a figure they knew all too well.

Figure: (menacingly) You dare to trespass in my domain. But you will not leave here alive.

With a cold laugh, the figure lunged forward, its eyes gleaming with malice. And in that moment, the group knew that their lives hung in the balance, their fate bound to the shadows of the past.

the group facing their greatest challenge yet, their courage and love tested in the face of unimaginable danger. As they prepare to confront the darkness that surrounds them, they know that only by standing together can they hope to emerge from the shadows unscathed.

The Dance of Shadows

The chamber echoed with the ominous laughter of the shadowy figure, its presence casting a chill over the group as they stood frozen in fear. In the flickering light of the torches, its form seemed to shift and warp, a sinister dance of darkness and despair.

Ria: (voice trembling) Who... who are you?

The figure's laughter echoed off the walls, sending shivers down their spines.

Figure: (sinisterly) I am the keeper of this place, the guardian of its secrets. And you... you are intruders in my domain.

Advik: (stepping forward, determination in his eyes) We mean you no harm. We're just trying to uncover the truth.

But the figure's laughter only grew louder, its malevolent gaze fixed upon them like a predator stalking its prey.

Figure: (mockingly) The truth? You think you can handle the truth? You know nothing of the darkness that lurks within these walls.

With a wave of its hand, the figure summoned shadows that twisted and writhed around them, threatening to engulf them in their suffocating embrace.

Hazel: (clinging to Dev) We have to get out of here!

Dev: (pulling her close) We will. We just have to stay together.

With a collective effort, the group fought back against the encroaching darkness, their hearts filled with determination and resolve. But as the shadows closed in around them, they knew that their strength alone would not be enough to overcome the darkness that threatened to consume them.

Marcas: (eyes darting around the chamber) There has to be a way out. We just have to find it.

Ava: (spotting a faint glimmer of light) Look! Over there!

With renewed hope, they followed the faint light, their footsteps echoing in the cavernous chamber. And as they drew closer to the source of the light, they realized that their salvation lay within reach—a narrow passage leading to freedom.

Ria: (breathlessly) This way! Hurry!

With one last effort, they raced towards the light, their hearts pounding with anticipation. And as they emerged from the chamber into the cool night air, they knew that they had faced the darkness and emerged victorious, their bond stronger than ever before.

But even as they caught their breath and celebrated their victory, they knew that their journey was far from over. For the shadows that lurked within the haunted house were but a glimpse of the darkness that lay beyond, and they knew that only by standing together could they hope to face the challenges that awaited them in the days to come.

And so, hand in hand, they walked into the night, ready to face whatever trials and tribulations lay ahead, their hearts filled with courage and their spirits unbreakable. For they knew that as long as they had each other, they could overcome any obstacle, no matter how daunting or insurmountable.

And so, their adventure continued, their bond forged in the fires of adversity, their love a beacon of light in the darkest of nights. And as they faced the challenges that lay ahead, they knew that they would always be stronger together, their hearts forever entwined in the dance of shadows.

CHAPTER XV

Respite in the Shadows

After their harrowing escape from the clutches of darkness, the group found themselves in a chamber deep within the haunted house. Despite the lingering tension in the air, they couldn't help but feel a sense of relief wash over them as they collapsed onto the dusty floor, their bodies weary from the trials they had faced.

Ria: (exhaling deeply) I think we're safe for now.

Advik: (nodding) Agreed. But we can't let our guard down just yet.

As they caught their breath and took stock of their surroundings, Hazel's stomach growled loudly, breaking the silence and eliciting a round of nervous laughter from the group.

Hazel: (sheepishly) Sorry... I guess I'm just really hungry.

Dev: (smiling) Don't worry, Hazel. We're all feeling it. We haven't eaten since... well, I don't even remember when.

Ava: (thoughtfully) What about our families? They must be worried sick about us.

The mention of their families brought a pang of guilt to the group, reminding them of the loved ones they had left behind in their quest for answers.

Marcas: (sighing) I wish we could just call them and let them know we're okay.

Ria: (placing a comforting hand on Marcas's shoulder) We'll find a way to let them know we're safe. But right now, we need to focus on getting out of here.

With a collective nod, the group set about making themselves as comfortable as possible in the dimly lit chamber. They gathered what little provisions they had and shared them amongst themselves, their hunger momentarily forgotten as they focused on replenishing their strength for the journey ahead.

As they settled in for the night, their thoughts turned to their families, their hearts heavy with the weight of their absence. But even in the midst of uncertainty and fear, they found solace in the knowledge that they were not alone—that they had each other to lean on and support through the darkest of times.

And so, as they drifted off to sleep amidst the shadows of the haunted house, their dreams were filled with visions of home and hearth, their hopes renewed by the promise of a brighter tomorrow. For they knew that no matter what challenges lay ahead, they would face them together, their bond stronger than any darkness that dared to threaten their unity.

Echoes of the Past

As the group rested in the chamber, a sense of unease lingered in the air, overshadowing their brief respite. Dreams of their families haunted their sleep, reminding them of the loved ones they had left behind in their quest for answers.

Ria: (stirring awake, her brow furrowed with worry) I can't shake this feeling... like something's not right.

Advik: (gently) It's just the stress getting to you, Ria. We're all feeling it.

But Ria couldn't shake the sense of foreboding that weighed heavily on her heart. Rising from her makeshift bed, she wandered to the chamber's entrance, her senses on high alert for any sign of danger.

Hazel: (noticing Ria's unease) What's wrong?

Ria: (voice barely above a whisper) I don't know... I just have this feeling that we're being watched.

The group exchanged worried glances, their nerves on edge as they listened for any hint of movement in the darkness.

Dev: (clenching his fists) We can't stay here. We need to keep moving.

With a collective nod, the group gathered their belongings and prepared to leave the chamber behind. But as they turned to go, a sudden noise echoed through the chamber—a faint whisper, barely audible above the sound of their own breathing.

Ava: (shivering) Did you hear that?

Marcas: (listening intently) It sounded like... voices.

The group fell silent, their senses on high alert as they strained to hear the whispers that echoed through the chamber. And as the voices grew louder, they realized with growing dread that they were not alone—that something sinister lurked in the shadows, waiting to reveal itself.

Ria: (voice trembling) We need to get out of here. Now.

With a sense of urgency, the group hurried from the chamber, their hearts pounding with fear as they fled into the darkness. But even as they ran, the whispers followed them, a haunting reminder of the darkness that lurked within the haunted house.

And as they emerged into the cold night air, they knew that their journey was far from over—that the echoes of the past would continue to haunt them until they uncovered the truth that lay hidden in the shadows.

the group fleeing from the chamber, their hearts heavy with the weight of the whispers that echoed in their ears. As they venture deeper into the darkness, they know that their quest for answers has only just begun—and that the dangers they face are greater than they ever imagined.

CHAPTER XVI

Network of Riddles

As the group delved deeper into the heart of the haunted house, they encountered a series of perplexing puzzles that guarded their path like silent watcher. Each challenge tested their intellect and resolve, pushing them to their limits as they sought to unravel the mysteries that lay before them.

The Symbolic Code:

In a dimly lit corridor, the walls were adorned with a mosaic of ancient symbols, their meaning lost to the passage of time. As the group studied the complicated patterns, they realized that the symbols held the key to unlocking the next stage of their journey. But decode the code would not be easy—it required keen observation and careful analysis.

Ria: (examining the symbols) These symbols seem to be arranged in a specific order, but I can't make sense of it.

Hazel: (joining Ria) Maybe there's a pattern to the arrangement. Let's see if we can figure it out.

Together, they studied the symbols, searching for any hint of order amidst the chaos. After much deliberation, they noticed a subtle repetition in the placement of certain symbols—a pattern that seemed to guide their arrangement.

Advik: (excitedly) I think we've got it! If we rearrange the symbols according to this pattern, it might unlock the next passage.

With renewed determination, the group set to work, carefully rearranging the symbols according to the pattern they had discovered. And as they did, the once unreadable code began to take shape, revealing a hidden message that pointed the way forward.

The Mirror Maze:

In the next chamber, they encountered a complex of mirrors that stretched on endlessly in every direction. The reflections seemed to warp and twist, leading them into problem at every turn. But amidst the confusion, they spotted subtle clues hidden within the reflections—hints that pointed to the correct path through the maze.

Dev: (studying the mirrors) The reflections seem to be shifting... but there's something different about that one.

Marcas: (following Dev's gaze) You're right! It's like there's a distortion in the reflection. Maybe that's the way out.

With cautious steps, they followed the distorted reflection, navigating the maze with care as they avoided the false leads that threatened to trap them forever. And after what felt like an eternity, they emerged from the maze victorious, their minds sharp and their resolve unshaken.

The Riddle of the Sphinx:

In the grand hall beyond the maze, they encountered a statue of a stone sphinx, its gaze fixed upon them with an air of challenge. As they approached, the sphinx spoke in a voice that echoed through the chamber, posing a series of riddles that tested their wit and wisdom.

Sphinx: "I speak without a mouth and hear without ears. I have no body, but I come alive with wind. What am I?"

Ria: (pondering the riddle) It's a... an echo!

The sphinx's eyes gleamed with approval as Ria answered correctly, but the challenges were far from over. With each riddle they solved, the sphinx revealed another, each one more fiendish than the last. But the group refused to be daunted, drawing on their collective knowledge and ingenuity to overcome every obstacle in their path.

As the group ventured deeper into the haunted house, they encountered a door unlike any they had seen before—a massive stone barrier secured by an intricate puzzle lock. The lock consisted of a series of interlocking gears, each adorned with cryptic symbols and mechanisms that seemed to shift and change with every turn.

Ria: (examining the lock) This is... complicated. I've never seen anything like it.

Advik: (frowning) It looks like some kind of puzzle. But how are we supposed to solve it?

The group gathered around the lock, their minds racing as they studied its intricate design. With each passing moment, the tension in the air grew, the weight of their uncertainty pressing down upon them like a heavy burden.

Hazel: (pointing to a series of symbols on one of the gears) Maybe these symbols hold the key to unlocking the puzzle.

Dev: (nodding) It's worth a try. Let's see if we can decipher their meaning.

With determination in their hearts, they set to work, carefully studying the symbols and searching for any hint of a pattern. But as they worked, they soon realized that the puzzle was far more complex than they had initially thought.

Marcas: (frustrated) It's like the symbols keep shifting... I can't make sense of it.

Ava: (studying the symbols intently) Maybe there's a clue hidden somewhere in the room. We just have to find it.

With renewed purpose, the group searched the chamber for any sign of a clue—a hidden message or symbol that might shed light on the puzzle before them. And as they searched, their efforts were rewarded with a faint glimmer of hope—a small inscription etched into the stone floor beneath their feet.

Ria: (reading the inscription aloud) "Only by aligning the symbols with the elements of nature can the lock be opened."

Advik: (pondering the inscription) The elements of nature... like earth, air, fire, and water?

Hazel: (excitedly) It's worth a try! Let's see if aligning the symbols with the elements unlocks the puzzle.

With a sense of determination, they returned to the lock, their minds focused on the task at hand. Carefully, they began to manipulate the gears, aligning the symbols with the elements of nature as they had deciphered from the inscription.

As they worked, the gears began to turn and shift, each movement bringing them closer to unlocking the puzzle. And with one final twist, the lock clicked into place, the door swinging open to reveal the chamber beyond.

With a collective sigh of relief, the group stepped through the doorway, their minds buzzing with the thrill of their victory. But as they ventured deeper into the depths of the haunted house, they knew that greater challenges lay ahead—challenges that would test their courage and determination to the limit.

But for now, they allowed themselves a moment of celebration, knowing that together, they could overcome any obstacle that stood in their way. And with their spirits high and their resolve unshaken, they pressed on into the unknown, ready to face whatever trials awaited them in the shadows.

Shadows of Concern

As the group continued their journey through the haunted house, a sense of unease lingered in the air, overshadowing their recent victory. Marcas, in particular, couldn't shake the feeling of concern that tourchered at him, his thoughts consumed by worry for Ava.

Marcas: (approaching Ava, his voice filled with concern) Ava, are you okay?

Ava: (forcing a smile) I'm fine, Marcas. Just a little tired, that's all.

But Marcas could see past her facade, his intuition telling him that something was amiss. He knew Ava better than anyone—knew the strength and resilience that lay beneath her cheerful exterior. And now, seeing her struggle, he couldn't help but feel a pang of worry in his heart.

Marcas: (placing a hand on Ava's shoulder) You don't have to pretend with me, Ava. I can tell when something's wrong.

Ava's smile faltered, her facade crumbling in the face of Marcas's unwavering concern. With a heavy sigh, she leaned into his touch, her shoulders sagging with the weight of her worries.

Ava: (softly) It's just... everything. This place, these challenges... it's all so overwhelming.

Marcas: (squeezing her shoulder gently) I know, Ava. But we're in this together. You don't have to face it alone.

With Marcas's words of comfort, Ava felt a glimmer of hope flicker to life within her. For so long, she had shouldered her burdens in silence, afraid to burden others with her troubles. But now, in the darkness of the haunted house, she realized that she didn't have to face her fears alone—that she had friends who cared for her, who would stand by her side no matter what.

Ava: (tears welling in her eyes) Thank you, Marcas. I don't know what I would do without you.

Marcas: (smiling reassuringly) You'll never have to find out, Ava. I'll always be here for you, no matter what.

As they shared a moment of quiet understanding, the rest of the group gathered around them, their expressions filled with concern and unity. And in that moment, surrounded by friends who cared for her, Ava knew that she could face whatever challenges lay ahead, her fears held at bay by the unwavering support of those she held dear.

CHAPTER XVII

Into the Depth

As the group frantically searched for a way to rescue Marcas from the abyss, Ava's heart pounded with fear and desperation. But amidst the chaos, another emotion simmered beneath the surface—a feeling she had long kept hidden, buried deep within her heart.

Ava watched with bated breath as her friends descended into the darkness, their voices fading into the abyss below. And as she waited, her thoughts turned to Marcas—her steadfast companion, her rock in times of trouble.

But as the seconds stretched into eternity, a new realization dawned on Ava—a truth she had long denied, even to herself. With every passing moment, her feelings for Marcas grew stronger, a love that dared not speak its name.

Hazel: (placing a comforting hand on Ava's shoulder) Ava, are you okay?

Ava forced a smile, her heart heavy with the weight of her unspoken emotions.

Ava: (forcing a smile) I'm fine, Hazel. Just... worried about Marcas, that's all.

But Hazel saw through her facade, her eyes filled with understanding.

Hazel: (softly) You care about him a lot, don't you?

Ava nodded, her voice barely above a whisper.

Ava: (tears welling in her eyes) More than anything. But... I can't tell him. Not now, when he's in danger. It wouldn't be fair.

Hazel squeezed Ava's hand reassuringly, her silent support a balm to her wounded heart.

Hazel: (gentle) Sometimes, love finds a way, Ava. Even in the darkest of times.

With Hazel's words echoing in her mind, Ava watched as her friends emerged from the Abyss, Marcas battered but alive. Relief washed over her, but beneath it all, her feelings for Marcas burned brighter than ever, a flame that refused to be extinguished.

As they continued their journey through the haunted house, Ava vowed to cherish every moment with Marcas, even if it meant keeping her feelings hidden away in the shadows of her heart. For now, their friendship was enough—a beacon of light in the darkness that surrounded them, guiding them through the perils that lay ahead.

A RAY OF HOPE

Exhausted and weary from their ordeal in the abyss, the group stumbled forward, their strength waning with each passing moment. The weight of their fear and uncertainty bore down upon them like a heavy burden, threatening to crush their spirits beneath its oppressive weight.

Ria: (voice strained) I don't know how much longer I can go on...

Hazel: (breathless) Me neither... I feel like I'm running on empty.

Ava: (sagging against the wall) We can't give up now. We have to keep moving.

But even as they forced themselves to press on, their bodies protested with every step, their muscles aching with fatigue. And as they trudged forward, their minds clouded with exhaustion, a glimmer of hope emerged from an unexpected source.

Dev: (searching through his bag) Wait a minute... I think I found something.

Advik: (perking up) What is it?

Dev's hands emerged from his bag, clutching a small bundle wrapped in cloth. With trembling fingers, he unwrapped the bundle, revealing a cache of food that they had packed for their journey.

Dev: (eyes widening) It's food! We have food in our bags!

Advik's eyes lit up with newfound energy as he reached for the provisions, his hunger forgotten in the face of their desperate need.

Advik: (smiling broadly) This is just what we need. Come on, let's eat.

With renewed vigor, the group gathered around Dev and Advik, their spirits lifted by the prospect of sustenance after so many hours without food. They shared the meager provisions amongst themselves, savoring each bite as if it were a feast fit for kings.

Ria: (sighing with relief) I feel so much better now.

Hazel: (smiling) Me too. I can't believe we almost forgot we had food with us.

Ava: (nodding) It's like a ray of hope in the darkness.

As they ate, their strength began to return, fueled by the nourishment of the food and the comradeship of their companions. And with each passing moment, their resolve grew stronger, their determination unshakeable in the face of the challenges that lay ahead.

With their bellies full and their spirits renewed, the group set out once more, their footsteps light and their hearts filled with hope. For even in the darkest of times, they knew that as long as they stood together, they could overcome any obstacle that stood in their way. And so, with their eyes set on the horizon and their minds focused on the journey ahead, they pressed forward into the unknown, ready to face whatever trials awaited them with courage and determination

47

CHAPTER XVIII

The Veil of Deception

As the group continued their journey through the haunted house, a sense of unease lingered in the air, casting a shadow over their newfound hope. The corridors twisted and turned, the darkness pressing in around them like a suffocating blanket.

Dev: (voice low) Something doesn't feel right...

Advik: (nodding) I agree. It's like the walls are closing in on us.

The group pressed forward, their senses on high alert for any sign of danger. But as they ventured deeper into the darkness, they realized with growing dread that they were not alone—that something sinister lurked in the shadows, waiting to reveal itself.

Ria: (whispering) Did you hear that?

Hazel: (tense) Hear what?

But before Hazel could respond, a voice echoed through the corridor—a chilling whisper that sent shivers down their spines.

Voice: "Beware the shadows, for they hide the truth."

Ava: (clutching her friends' arms) What was that?

Marcas: (grim) I don't know, but we need to keep moving. We can't stay here.

With a sense of urgency, the group pressed on, their hearts pounding with fear as they navigated the twisting corridors. But with each step forward, the darkness seemed to grow deeper, the shadows closing in around them like grasping claws.

And then, they saw it—a figure lurking in the darkness, its eyes gleaming with malice as it emerged from the shadows.

Ria: (voice trembling) What... what is that?

Advik: (stepping forward) Stay back! We won't let you harm us.

But as they prepared to defend themselves, the figure spoke, its voice filled with a strange mixture of sorrow and longing.

Figure: "Wait! Please, you must listen to me."

The group hesitated, unsure of what to do. But as they gazed into the figure's eyes, they saw a glimmer of humanity—a flicker of pain and regret that tugged at their hearts.

Hazel: (tentatively) Who are you?

Figure: (lowering its head) I am but a lost soul, trapped within these walls. Please, you must help me.

With a sense of compassion, the group approached the figure, their fear giving way to curiosity.

Ria: (softening) What do you need?

Figure: (pleading) There is a way to break the curse that binds me to this place. But I cannot do it alone. You must help me find the key.

As the figure spoke, a glimmer of hope ignited within the group—a chance to break free from the darkness that threatened to consume them. And with a newfound sense of purpose, they vowed to help the lost soul find the key to its freedom, no matter the cost.

With their hearts united in their quest, the group set out once more, their eyes set on the horizon and their minds focused on the journey ahead. For even in the darkest of times, they knew that as long as they stood together, they could overcome any obstacle that stood in their way. And so, with courage in their hearts and hope in their souls, they pressed forward into the unknown, ready to face whatever trials awaited them with unwavering resolve.

The Key to Freedom

Determined to help the lost soul find the key to its freedom, the group pressed forward through the haunted corridors, their senses alert for any sign of the elusive artifact. The air hung heavy with tension, each step fraught with uncertainty as they navigated the labyrinthine passages.

Dev: (scanning their surroundings) Keep your eyes peeled, everyone. The key could be anywhere.

Advik: (nodding) Agreed. We need to search every nook and cranny until we find it.

With their resolve unyielding, they scoured the chamber, their hands brushing against cold stone walls as they searched for any sign of the key. But as time passed and their efforts yielded no results, doubt began to creep into their minds, casting a shadow over their hopes of finding the elusive artifact.

Ava: (voice tinged with frustration) This is hopeless. We've been searching for hours and found nothing.

Hazel: (placing a reassuring hand on Ava's shoulder) Don't lose hope, Ava. We'll find the key, I know it.

But even as Hazel spoke, the weight of their failure hung heavy in the air, threatening to crush their spirits beneath its oppressive weight. And yet, just when it seemed that all hope was lost, a glimmer of light appeared in the darkness—a faint flicker of movement caught in the corner of their eyes.

Ria: (pointing) Look! Over there!

Their hearts leapt with hope as they rushed toward the source of the movement, their eyes widening with wonder as they beheld a small alcove hidden in the shadows. And within the alcove lay the object of their search—the key to the lost soul's freedom.

Marcas: (reaching for the key) We found it! The key!

With trembling hands, Marcas retrieved the key from its resting place, the metal cool against his skin as he held it aloft. And as he did, a sense of anticipation filled the chamber, as if the very air itself held its breath in anticipation of what was to come.

Figure: (voice echoing through the chamber) At last... the key to my freedom.

The group turned to see the lost soul standing before them, its form wavering in the dim light of the chamber. And as they watched, the figure reached out a hand, its fingers brushing against the key with a sense of longing.

Figure: (voice filled with gratitude) Thank you, brave souls, for your kindness and courage. With this key, I can finally be free.

With a sense of reverence, Marcas placed the key into the figure's outstretched hand, his heart filled with a mixture of sadness and hope. And as the figure grasped the key tightly, a brilliant light engulfed the chamber, illuminating the darkness with its radiant glow.

And then, in an instant, the figure was gone—vanished into thin air, leaving behind only a sense of peace and gratitude in its wake. The group watched in awe as the light faded, the chamber returning to its silent vigil as if nothing had happened.

But amidst the stillness, a sense of satisfaction filled their hearts, knowing that they had helped a lost soul find its way home. And as they stood together in the fading light, they knew that their journey was far from over—but with each challenge they faced, they would face it together, their bond stronger than ever before.

CHAPTER XIX

Echoes of the Past

As the group continued their journey through the haunted house, a newfound sense of purpose filled their hearts, buoyed by their recent success in helping the lost soul find its freedom. Yet, amidst the lingering echoes of their triumph, a shadow of doubt still loomed, reminding them that their quest was far from over.

Hazel: (voice echoing in the chamber) I can't shake the feeling that there's more to this place than meets the eye.

Ria: (nodding) Agreed. It's like there are secrets hidden within these walls, waiting to be uncovered.

Their words hung heavy in the air, the silence of the chamber amplifying the weight of their thoughts. But before they could dwell further on their musings, a faint sound reached their ears—a soft, haunting melody that seemed to emanate from the very stones themselves.

Ava: (listening intently) Do you hear that?

Advik: (straining to hear) It sounds like... music.

With a sense of curiosity, the group followed the sound of the music, their footsteps echoing through the empty corridors as they searched for its source. And then, at last, they found it—a grand hall bathed in moonlight, its walls adorned with faded tapestries and crumbling statues.

Marcas: (in awe) It's beautiful... but where is the music coming from?

As if in response to his question, a figure emerged from the shadows—a ghostly apparition with ethereal features and eyes that seemed to hold the wisdom of centuries.

Ghost: (voice echoing in the chamber) Welcome, travelers, to the Hall of Echoes.

The group watched in wonder as the ghostly figure beckoned them forward, its presence both comforting and unnerving in equal measure.

Hazel: (voice trembling) Who... who are you?

Ghost: (smiling sadly) I am but a memory—a remnant of a time long past. I have watched over this hall for centuries, waiting for those who would seek the truth hidden within its walls.

Ria: (curious) What truth?

The ghost's smile faded, replaced by a look of solemn determination.

Ghost: (voice echoing) The truth of what happened here—the secrets buried beneath the sands of time. You have been chosen to uncover the mysteries of this place, to bring light to the darkness that shrouds its history.

With a sense of purpose burning in their hearts, the group listened as the ghost recounted the tale of the haunted house—a story of betrayal, tragedy, and redemption, woven into the very fabric of its walls.

As the ghost spoke, the chamber seemed to come alive with the echoes of the past, the music of bygone days filling the air with its haunting melody. And as the group listened, they knew that their journey was far from over—that with each step forward, they would uncover new truths and face new challenges, their courage and determination guiding them through the darkness that lay ahead.

Shadows of the Past

As the group listened to the ghost's tale, they were transported back in time to a bygone era—a time when the land upon which the haunted house stood was teeming with life and vitality. But beneath the surface, a darkness lurked, waiting to be unleashed upon the unsuspecting world.

Centuries ago, the land was ruled by a powerful nobleman—a man of wealth and influence, whose name struck fear into the hearts of all who dared to defy him. But behind his facade of power and prestige lay a dark secret—a secret that would ultimately seal the fate of all who crossed his path.

The nobleman's lust for power knew no bounds, and he would stop at nothing to achieve his goals. And so, when rumors began to spread of a hidden treasure buried deep within the earth, he saw it as an opportunity to further his own ambitions.

With a ruthless determination, the nobleman ordered the construction of a grand estate upon the very spot where the treasure was said to lie, believing that by claiming the treasure for himself, he could solidify his grip on power and ensure his legacy for generations to come.

But as the grand estate took shape, whispers of discontent began to spread among the common folk, who feared the nobleman's insatiable greed and the darkness that seemed to follow in his wake. And as tensions reached a boiling point, a rebellion erupted—a desperate attempt to overthrow the tyrant and reclaim what was rightfully theirs.

The nobleman, sensing the threat to his power, unleashed a wave of terror upon the land, unleashing his forces upon the unsuspecting populace with a fury unmatched by any other. And in the chaos that followed, the grand estate became a symbol of the nobleman's tyranny—a monument to the suffering of those who dared to defy him.

But amidst the confusion, a glimmer of hope remained—a small band of rebels who refused to bow to the nobleman's will, their courage and determination shining like a beacon in the darkness. And as they fought to reclaim their freedom, they vowed to uncover the truth behind the haunted house and put an end to the nobleman's reign of terror once and for all.

As the ghost's tale came to an end, the group stood in awe of the history that lay hidden within the walls of the haunted house. And as they prepared to continue their journey, they knew that their quest had taken on a new significance—that they were not just searching for answers, but fighting for justice and redemption in a world consumed by darkness.

CHAPTER XX

Threads of Fate

As the group absorbed the haunting tale of the nobleman and the rebellion that shook the land centuries ago, a sense of unease settled over them. But amidst the shadows of the past, a new revelation emerged—a connection that bound their present to the distant echoes of history.

hazel: (voice filled with wonder) This story... it's like something out of a legend.

Ria: (nodding) But there's something more to it, something we haven't uncovered yet.

Advik: (thoughtfully) I can't shake the feeling that there's a reason we were drawn to this place, that our destinies are intertwined with its history.

Ava: (eyes wide with realization) What if... what if there's a link between the nobleman and Prisha's grandfather?

The group fell silent, their minds racing with the implications of Ava's revelation. Could it be possible that Prisha's family history was somehow connected to the dark secrets buried within the haunted house?

marcas: (voice tinged with urgency) We need to find out more about Prisha's family history. There may be clues that could help us unravel the mysteries of this place.

With a sense of purpose burning in their hearts, the group set out to investigate Prisha's family history, scouring ancient records and dusty tomes for any sign of a connection to the nobleman who had once ruled the land with an iron fist.

And then, at last, they found it—a faded manuscript detailing the lineage of Prisha's family, tracing their ancestry back through the generations to a time when the nobleman's reign of terror was at its peak.

hazel: (reading aloud) "Prisha's grandfather... he was a key figure in the rebellion against the nobleman. He fought valiantly to overthrow the tyrant and reclaim the land for the people."

Ria: (eyes wide with realization) So that's why Prisha's family has always been drawn to this place. They're connected to its history in ways they never knew.

As the pieces of the puzzle fell into place, the group's resolve strengthened, their determination unyielding in the face of the challenges that lay ahead. For now, they knew that their quest had taken on a new significance—that they were not just seeking answers, but fighting for justice and redemption in a story that spanned centuries.

And as they prepared to continue their journey, they vowed to uncover the truth behind the haunted house and put an end to the darkness that had plagued the land for far too long. For they knew that their destinies were intertwined with the echoes of the past, and that only by confronting the shadows head-on could they hope to find the light that would lead them to victory.

Shadows of Peril

As the group delved deeper into the haunted house, their path fraught with danger, they encountered perils unlike any they had faced before. The air grew heavy with tension, every step forward a battle against the darkness that threatened to engulf them.

Dev: (voice strained) Watch your step, everyone. These corridors are treacherous.

Advik: (eyes darting around) I don't like the look of this place. It feels... wrong.

Their words hung in the air, a silent acknowledgment of the dangers that lurked around every corner. And as they pressed forward, their senses on high alert, they soon found themselves facing a series of challenges that tested their courage and resolve.

First, they encountered a maze of twisting corridors, each path leading deeper into the heart of the haunted house. With no clear way forward, they were forced to rely on their instincts and intuition to guide them through the labyrinthine passages, their nerves fraying with each dead end they encountered.

Then, they stumbled upon a series of traps—hidden pitfalls and tripwires that threatened to ensnare them at every turn. With quick reflexes and steady nerves, they navigated the perilous obstacles, their hearts pounding with adrenaline as they narrowly avoided disaster time and time again.

But perhaps the greatest peril of all was the darkness that seemed to seep into their very souls, whispering of untold horrors and unseen dangers lurking just beyond the edge of perception. It was a darkness that threatened to consume them whole, to strip away their courage and leave them lost and alone in the depths of the haunted house.

Ria: (voice trembling) I don't know how much longer I can do this. It feels like we're fighting a losing battle.

hazel: (placing a reassuring hand on Ria's shoulder) Don't give up, Ria. We're in this together, remember?

Ria looked into hazel's eyes, her gaze filled with an unspoken gratitude and admiration.

Ria: (softly) Thank you, hazel. For everything. Your friendship means more to me than you'll ever know.

hazel's eyes filled with tears at Ria's heartfelt words, her own heart swelling with love and gratitude for her dear friend.

hazel: (emotionally) And you, Ria. Your strength and courage inspire me every day. I don't know where I'd be without you.

With their bond stronger than ever before, the group pressed forward, their hearts united in their quest to uncover the truth behind the haunted house. For even in the face of the greatest perils, they knew that as long as they stood together, they could overcome any obstacle that stood in their way. And so, with courage in their hearts and love in their souls, they forged ahead into the unknown, ready to face whatever challenges lay ahead with unwavering resolve.

CHAPTER XXI

Moments of Light

After facing the perils of the haunted house, the group finally reached a safe haven—a quiet chamber hidden away from the darkness that lurked beyond its walls. Exhausted but relieved, they took refuge in the sanctuary of the chamber, grateful for the chance to rest and recuperate after their harrowing journey.

As they settled in for the night, a sense of camaraderie filled the air, the tension of their ordeal melting away in the warmth of their companionship. And amidst the flickering glow of torchlight, they shared tales and laughter, their spirits buoyed by the promise of a momentary respite from the shadows that threatened to consume them.

Marcas: (stretching out on the floor) Ah, it feels good to finally take a break.

Advik: (grinning) You said it. I don't know about you guys, but I could use a good night's sleep.

Dev: (nodding) Agreed. We've been through a lot today.

As they settled in for the night, they took turns regaling each other with stories and jokes, their laughter echoing through the chamber like music in the darkness. And amidst the lighthearted banter, they found solace in each other's company, their bonds of friendship growing stronger with each passing moment.

Ria: (teasing) Hey Dev, remember that time you tripped over your own feet and fell into that pile of leaves?

Dev: (rolling his eyes) Oh please, Ria. Let's not bring that up again.

Hazel: (chuckling) And Advik, remember when you tried to impress that girl by doing a backflip and ended up landing on your face instead?

Advik: (grinning sheepishly) Hey, we agreed never to speak of that again.

Ava: (joining in) And Marcas, remember when you accidentally set fire to your eyebrows during chemistry class?

Marcas: (blushing) Okay, okay. Let's not dwell on the past, shall we?

As they shared jokes and stories late into the night, their laughter filled the chamber with a warmth and light that banished the shadows that lingered in the corners. And amidst the laughter and camaraderie, they found comfort in the knowledge that no matter what trials lay ahead, they would face them together, their bonds of friendship and love stronger than ever before.

Comfort in the Night

As the night wore on and the others drifted into sleep, Ria found herself unable to find rest, her mind consumed by worry and guilt. She tossed and turned on her makeshift bed, the weight of her fears pressing down upon her like a leaden blanket.

Advik: (softly) Ria? Are you alright?

Ria looked up to see Advik standing beside her, his concern etched upon his face like a shadow in the moonlight.

Ria: (voice trembling) I... I can't sleep, Advik. What if something happens to us? What if I've led us into danger?

Advik: (placing a reassuring hand on her shoulder) Hey, don't worry about that. We're in this together, remember? And no matter what happens, we'll face it as a team.

Ria's eyes overflowing with tears as she looked up at Advik, his words like a guiding of light in the darkness.

Ria: (voice choked with emotion) Thank you, Advik. I don't know what I'd do without you.

With a gentle smile, Advik pulled Ria into a comforting embrace, his warmth and strength wrapping around her like a protective cloak. And in that moment, all of Ria's fears melted away, replaced by a sense of peace and security in Advik's arms.

But their tender moment was soon interrupted by the playful teasing of their friends, who had been awakened by their whispers.

Dev: (teasingly) Oh my god, lovebirds got some time alone, huh?

Hazel: (chuckling) Dev, stop it. Ria, come here. Sleep with me.

Hazel reached out to Ria, pulling her into a tight embrace and soothing her fears with her comforting presence.

Meanwhile, Dev turned to Advik with a mischievous grin.

Dev: (mockingly) Hey Advik, need a cuddle buddy?

Advik shot Dev a playful glare, his cheeks flushing with embarrassment.

Advik: (jokingly) No thanks, Dev. I think I'll pass.

Dev: See man! Marcas and Ava are in deep sleep.

Advik: Dont disturb them buddy, let them sleep.

With laughter and light-hearted teasing filling the air, the group settled back into their makeshift beds, their bonds of friendship and love stronger than ever before. And as they drifted off to sleep, they knew that no matter what trials lay ahead, they would face them together, their hearts united in a bond that could withstand even the darkest of nights.

CHAPTER XXII

Whispers in the Dark

As dawn broke over the horizon, the group stirred from their slumber, the events of the previous night still fresh in their minds. But as they prepared to continue their journey through the haunted house, a sense of foreboding hung heavy in the air, as if the shadows themselves were alive with malevolent intent.

Ria: (voice filled with apprehension) I don't like the feeling of this place. It's like... it's watching us.

Advik: (nodding) I know what you mean. It's like there's something lurking in the shadows, just waiting to pounce.

Their words echoed through the chamber, the silence of the morning broken only by the faint rustle of leaves outside. And as they ventured deeper into the darkness, they soon found themselves facing a new challenge—one that tested not only their courage, but their very sanity.

Whispers began to fill the air, soft and insistent, like the murmur of voices carried on the wind. At first, they seemed like nothing more than figments of their imagination, the product of tired minds and frayed nerves. But as the whispers grew louder, they realized with growing dread that they were not alone—that something sinister was at play in the depths of the haunted house.

Hazel: (voice trembling) Do you... do you hear that?

Ava: (nodding) It sounds like... voices.

With a sense of trepidation, they followed the sound of the whispers, their hearts pounding with fear as they ventured deeper into the darkness. And then, at last, they found it—a hidden chamber concealed behind a crumbling wall, its entrance obscured by centuries of dust and debris.

Marcas: (eyes wide with wonder) What... what is this place?

As they stepped into the chamber, they were greeted by a sight that sent shivers down their spines—a room filled with ancient relics and artifacts, their surfaces gleaming in the dim light of the torches.

But amidst the artifacts, they saw something else—something that filled them with a sense of unease. It was a statue—a grotesque figure with twisted features and eyes that seemed to follow them wherever they went.

Advik: (voice barely above a whisper) What... what is that?

No one had an answer, but as they gazed upon the statue, they felt a chill run down their spines—a primal fear that spoke of ancient evils and unspeakable horrors lurking just beyond the edge of their perception.

And as the whispers grew louder, echoing through the chamber like a cacophony of voices from the grave, the group knew that they had stumbled upon something far more sinister than they had ever imagined—a mystery that threatened to consume them whole if they dared to uncover its secrets.

The Unveiling

As the whispers echoed through the chamber, the group stood frozen in fear, their minds reeling with the weight of the mysteries that surrounded them. But amidst the darkness, a glimmer of determination flickered in their eyes, driving them forward in their quest for answers.

Ria: (voice trembling) We... we have to find out what's causing those whispers.

Advik: (nodding) Agreed. Whatever it is, it can't be good.

With their resolve strengthened, they set out to investigate the source of the whispers, their hearts pounding with anticipation as they delved deeper into the chamber. And then, at last, they found it—a hidden alcove tucked away in the darkest corner of the room.

Hazel: (voice barely above a whisper) What... what is this place?

The alcove was filled with strange symbols and markings, their meaning lost to time. But as they studied the symbols, they felt a sense of unease wash over them—a primal fear that whispered of ancient secrets and forbidden knowledge.

Marcas: (pointing) Look! There's something behind that wall.

With trembling hands, they began to chip away at the crumbling plaster, revealing a hidden passageway that led deeper into the darkness. And as they stepped through the narrow opening, they felt a chill run down their spines—a sense of foreboding that spoke of the dangers that lay ahead.

Ava: (voice filled with apprehension) I don't like the look of this.

But despite their misgivings, they pressed forward, driven by a desire to uncover the truth behind the whispers that haunted them. And as they ventured deeper into the passageway, they soon found themselves standing before a massive stone door, its surface etched with intricate carvings and symbols.

Ria: (breathless) This... this must be it. The source of the whispers.

With a sense of trepidation, they pushed open the stone door, revealing a chamber bathed in an eerie blue light. And there, in the center of the chamber, stood a figure cloaked in shadow—a being of pure malevolence that emanated a sense of dread unlike anything they had ever known.

Figure: (voice echoing through the chamber) Welcome, travelers, to the heart of darkness.

As the figure spoke, the chamber filled with a deafening silence, broken only by the sound of their own racing hearts. And as they gazed upon the figure before them, they knew that their journey had only just begun—that the true horrors of the haunted house had yet to reveal themselves, and that they stood on the brink of a darkness that threatened to consume them whole.

CHAPTER XXIII

Confrontation in the Shadows

The figure loomed before them, its presence casting a pall of darkness over the chamber. The group stood frozen, their hearts pounding with a mixture of fear and defiance as they faced the embodiment of the evil that had plagued them since their arrival.

Ria: (voice trembling) Who... what are you?

Figure: (voice echoing ominously) I am the keeper of this place—the guardian of its darkest secrets.

As the figure spoke, its form shifted and swirled, tendrils of shadow reaching out to ensnare them in its grasp. But despite the overwhelming sense of dread that filled the chamber, the group stood firm, their resolve unyielding in the face of the darkness that threatened to consume them.

Advik: (stepping forward) We're not afraid of you. Whatever you are, we'll stop you.

The figure's laughter echoed through the chamber, a sound that sent shivers down their spines.

Figure: (mockingly) Foolish mortals. You think you can defy me? You are nothing but insects crawling in the darkness, blind to the truth of your own insignificance.

But the group refused to back down, their determination burning brighter with each passing moment.

Dev: (voice filled with defiance) We may be small, but together, we're stronger than you'll ever know. And we won't let you destroy everything we hold dear.

The figure's laughter faded, replaced by a cold, calculating gaze that seemed to pierce through their very souls.

Figure: (voice dripping with malice) You dare to challenge me? Very well. Let us see if you have the strength to withstand the true power of the shadows.

With a wave of its hand, the figure unleashed a wave of darkness that engulfed the chamber, casting the group into a swirling abyss of terror and despair. But even as they struggled against the suffocating darkness, they refused to give in to despair, their bonds of friendship and love guiding them through the darkest of nights.

And as they stood together, united in their defiance against the forces of evil, they knew that no matter what trials lay ahead, they would face them with unwavering resolve. For in the heart of darkness, they had found the light of their own courage, and nothing in this world or the next could ever extinguish its flame.

Bonds of Love and Sacrifice

As the group navigated through the perilous depths of the haunted house, danger lurked around every corner, threatening to consume them in its malevolent grasp. And amidst the chaos and uncertainty, a moment of quiet tragedy unfolded, forever altering the course of their journey.

Hazel stumbled, her hand brushing against a jagged edge of stone, a sharp pain shooting through her fingers. But in the heat of the moment, she scarcely noticed the blood that welled up from the wound, her focus consumed by the pressing urgency of their quest.

Dev: (voice tinged with concern) Hazel, your hand... it's bleeding.

Hazel glanced down, her eyes widening in shock as she saw the crimson stain that marred her skin. With trembling hands, Dev quickly tore a strip of fabric from his shirt and bound it tightly around her wounded hand, his heart hammering with fear at the sight of her pain.

Meanwhile, Ria and Ava hovered nearby, their worry etched upon their faces as they watched over their injured friend. Advik and Marcas stood guard at the entrance to the chamber, their eyes scanning the shadows for any sign of the figure that lurked in the darkness.

But amidst the chaos and uncertainty, a moment of quiet intimacy unfolded between Dev and Hazel, their bond of love and sacrifice shining bright amidst the darkness that threatened to consume them.

Dev: (voice filled with emotion) Hazel, I... I love you. I will always be by your side, no matter what may come.

Hazel's eyes filled with tears at Dev's heartfelt words, her heart overflowing with love for the man who had stood by her through thick and thin.

Hazel: (voice choked with emotion) Dev, I... I love you too. And I will never leave your side, no matter what may happen.

With tears streaming down their cheeks, Dev knelt before Hazel, his hands trembling as he fashioned a makeshift ring from a scrap of paper. And as he slipped the ring onto her finger, a silent vow passed between them—a promise to stand together against the darkness, come what may.

Their friends looked on, their hearts swelling with emotion at the sight of the love that blossomed amidst the chaos and uncertainty of their journey. And as Dev and Hazel embraced, their love shining bright amidst the shadows, they knew that no matter what trials lay ahead, they would face them together, united in their unwavering bond of love and sacrifice.

CHAPTER XXIV

Shadows of Doubt

As the night wore on, the group huddled together in the safety of the chamber, their minds swirling with thoughts of the figure that lurked in the darkness beyond. But amidst their fear and uncertainty, a seed of doubt began to take root in their hearts—a nagging suspicion that not all was as it seemed.

Ria: (voice filled with concern) What if... what if we're wrong about the figure? What if it's not the true threat here?

Advik: (frowning) You mean... you think there's something else out there?

Ria nodded, her brow furrowed with worry.

Ria: (hesitantly) I don't know. But something doesn't feel right. We need to be cautious.

Her words hung in the air, a sobering reminder of the dangers that surrounded them. And as they debated their next course of action, a sense of unease settled over the chamber, casting a shadow of doubt over their once-unshakeable resolve.

Meanwhile, Dev and Hazel sat huddled together in the corner of the chamber, their hands intertwined as they sought solace in each other's embrace. But even amidst their love, a sense of fear lingered in the air—a fear of what the future might hold, and of the darkness that seemed to close in around them with each passing moment.

Dev: (voice barely above a whisper) Hazel, do you... do you think we'll make it out of here alive?

Hazel: (squeezing his hand) I don't know, Dev. But as long as we're together, we'll find a way to survive.

Their words were a balm to each other's souls, a reminder that even in the darkest of times, their love would light the way. But as they clung to each other amidst the shadows, they knew that their journey was far from over, and that the true test of their courage still lay ahead.

And so, as the night stretched on and the darkness pressed in around them, the group braced themselves for the trials that awaited them, their hearts united in their determination to face whatever horrors lurked in the depths of the haunted house. For even in the face of uncertainty, they knew that as long as they stood together, they would never falter in their quest for freedom and redemption.

Light of Hope

As the group pondered their next move, a glimmer of hope flickered in the darkness—a clue that promised to lead them out of the haunted house and into the light of safety once more.

Advik: (pointing to the wall) Look! There's something carved into the stone.

The others gathered around, their eyes widening in astonishment as they saw the faint outline of a symbol etched into the ancient stone.

Ria: (voice filled with excitement) It looks like... like a key!

Hazel: (nodding) Maybe it's a clue. A clue that could lead us out of here.

With renewed determination, they set out to decipher the meaning of the symbol, their minds racing with possibilities as they searched for a way to unlock the mysteries of the haunted house.

Marcas: (examining the symbol closely) I think I've seen this before. It's an ancient symbol of protection—a symbol that wards off evil and guides the way to safety.

Ava: (eyes alight with excitement) So you mean... you mean it's a way out?

Marcas nodded, his heart swelling with hope at the thought of finally escaping the darkness that had held them captive for so long.

Marcas: (determined) Yes. I believe it is. We just have to follow the path it lays out for us.

With their spirits lifted by the promise of freedom, they set out to follow the trail of clues that the symbol offered, their hearts filled with determination as they ventured deeper into the depths of the haunted house.

And as they followed the winding corridors and hidden passages, each step bringing them closer to the light of safety, they knew that their journey was far from over. But with the symbol as their guide, they faced the challenges that lay ahead with courage and resolve, their eyes fixed on the promise of a brighter tomorrow that awaited them beyond the darkness.

CHAPTER XXV

The Abyss Beckons

As the group pressed forward, their hopes buoyed by the promise of escape, they unwittingly stumbled upon a danger that threatened to engulf them all—a gaping chasm that yawned open before them like the jaws of some ancient beast.

Ria: (voice filled with dread) What... what is this?

Before them stretched a vast abyss, its depths shrouded in darkness, its edges crumbling and unstable. The group stood frozen on the precipice, their hearts pounding with fear as they realized the enormity of the danger that lay before them.

Advik: (voice trembling) We... we can't cross this. It's too dangerous.

Hazel: (frantically searching for a way out) There must be another way. We can't be trapped here forever.

But as they searched for an escape, they realized with growing horror that there was no easy path forward. The abyss seemed to stretch on endlessly, its depths unfathomable and its edges treacherous.

Dev: (voice tinged with desperation) What do we do now? We can't just stand here.

Marcas: (surveying the abyss) Maybe... maybe there's a way to bridge the gap. Some kind of rope or...

But before he could finish his sentence, a sudden rumbling filled the air, the ground beneath them shaking violently as if in protest.

Ava: (eyes wide with fear) What's happening?

With a deafening roar, the ground began to give way beneath them, the edges of the abyss crumbling and collapsing into the depths below. The group scmarcasbled to find purchase, their hearts racing as they teetered on the brink of disaster.

In a desperate bid for survival, they clung to each other, their hands linked in a chain of solidarity as they fought against the pull of the abyss. But as the ground continued to crumble beneath them, they knew that their strength alone would not be enough to save them from the chasm that threatened to swallow them whole.

With their lives hanging in the balance, they braced themselves for the final plunge into the abyss, their hearts united in a silent prayer for deliverance from the darkness that threatened to consume them. And as they stood on the edge of oblivion, they knew that only by facing their fears together could they hope to emerge from the depths and find the light of safety once more.

A Fight for Survival

As the ground crumbled beneath them, the group found themselves teetering on the edge of the abyss, their hearts pounding with fear as they fought to maintain their footing against the relentless pull of gravity.

Advik: (struggling to keep his balance) Hold on, everyone! We can't give up now!

With every ounce of strength they possessed, they clung to each other, their fingers digging into the crumbling earth as they fought against the inexorable force of the abyss. But try as they might, they could feel themselves slipping, inch by inch, closer to the yawning chasm below.

Ria: (voice trembling) We... we have to find a way out of this.

Hazel: (frantically searching for a solution) There must be something we can do!

But as they searched for an escape, their options grew ever more limited. The ground continued to crumble beneath them, the edges of the abyss drawing nearer with each passing moment.

Dev: (voice filled with desperation) We have to jump! It's our only chance!

With no other choice, the group made a split-second decision, their hearts pounding with adrenaline as they leaped into the unknown. And as they plummeted into the depths below, they braced themselves for the impact, their minds racing with the uncertainty of what lay ahead.

But even as they fell, a sense of unity filled the air, binding them together in their fight for survival. And as they landed with a bone-jarring thud on the other side of the abyss, they knew that they had faced their greatest challenge yet and emerged victorious.

With their hearts still racing and their bodies bruised but unbroken, they picked themselves up from the ground, their spirits buoyed by the knowledge that they had overcome the darkness that had threatened to consume them. And as they continued on their journey, they did so with a newfound sense of purpose, their bond of friendship stronger than ever before, forged in the crucible of adversity.

CHAPTER XXVI

The Struggle for Survival

As the group pressed onward, their spirits buoyed by their narrow escape from the abyss, a new challenge emerged—one that threatened to test their resolve like never before. With their food dwindling and the end of their supplies looming on the horizon, they found themselves faced with the stark reality of their situation.

Ria: (voice filled with concern) We... we only have four days of food left. And it's already been three days since we entered this place.

Advik: (frowning) We need to find a way to stretch our supplies until we can find a way out of here.

With each passing moment, the weight of their predicament bore down upon them, casting a shadow of uncertainty over their once-determined spirits. But even amidst the darkness, a glimmer of hope remained—a determination to fight for survival against all odds.

Ava: (voice trembling) I never thought it would come to this. But we have to stay strong, for each other.

Marcas: (placing a reassuring hand on Ava's shoulder) We've faced worse odds before, Ava. And we've always come out on top. We'll find a way through this, together.

Ava nodded, her eyes reflecting a mix of fear and determination as she clung to Marcas's words of encouragement. In the darkness of the night, with their stomachs empty and their future uncertain, their bond remained unshakeable, a beacon of hope in the face of adversity.

Hazel: (voice tinged with desperation) We have to ration our food carefully. We can't afford to waste a single morsel.

Dev: (nodding) Agreed. Every scrap counts.

With grim determination, they set about dividing their remaining supplies, portioning out their meager rations with care and precision. But even as they tried to make the most of what little they had, the specter of hunger loomed large in their minds, a constant reminder of the perilous path they walked.

As night fell once more, they huddled together in the darkness, their stomachs empty and their hearts heavy with the weight of their hunger. But even amidst their struggle, they found solace in the warmth of each other's company, their bond of friendship a beacon of hope in the face of despair.

And as they drifted off to sleep, their bodies weary but their spirits unbroken, they knew that the road ahead would be long and arduous. But with their lives hanging in the balance, they were determined to fight for survival with every ounce of strength they possessed, for in the depths of their darkest hour, they refused to let go of the flicker of hope that burned bright within their hearts.

As the group pressed onward, their hunger gnawing at their insides and their spirits flagging with each passing moment, a glimmer of hope appeared on the horizon—a faint light that beckoned them forward with the promise of salvation.

Marcas: (voice filled with determination) I can't... I can't find the truth in this darkness. Maybe... maybe it's better if we focus on getting out of here first. We can leave the mysteries behind us for now.

His words hung in the air, a silent acknowledgment of the challenges they faced and the uncertainty that lay ahead. But even amidst their doubts and fears, a sense of relief washed over them—a newfound clarity that urged them onward in their quest for freedom.

Advik: (nodding) He's right. Our priority should be finding a way out of here. Everything else can wait.

With renewed resolve, they set out once more, their eyes fixed on the distant light that shimmered in the darkness like a beacon of hope. But as they journeyed closer to their goal, they soon found themselves beset by a new set of obstacles—twisting corridors, hidden traps, and malevolent forces that seemed determined to thwart their every move.

Hazel: (voice filled with frustration) Why does it feel like everything is working against us?

Ria: (gritting her teeth) We can't give up now. We've come too far to turn back.

With each step forward, the challenges grew ever more daunting, testing their strength and resilience to their limits. But even as they stumbled and faltered, they refused to let go of the flicker of hope that burned bright within their hearts, driving them forward through the darkness toward the promise of a brighter tomorrow.

And as they pressed onward, their spirits bolstered by the knowledge that they faced the challenges together as one, they knew that no obstacle, no matter how insurmountable, could ever stand in the way of their unwavering determination to find their way out of the haunted house and into the light of freedom once more.

CHAPTER XXVII

Trusting the Path

Dev's words hung heavy in the air, his voice filled with a sense of conviction that resonated with each member of the group. As they stood at the crossroads, with their path forward shrouded in uncertainty, a newfound sense of purpose stirred within them.

Dev: (voice firm) We can't go back. And we can't afford to stand still. We have to trust that there's a reason we're being guided this way. We need to keep moving forward, no matter what.

His words were met with nods of agreement from the others, their resolve hardened by the trials they had faced and the challenges that lay ahead. With each step forward, they felt a sense of clarity wash over them, as if the darkness itself were parting to reveal the path they were meant to follow.

Ria: (determined) He's right. We have to trust in ourselves and in each other. We'll find a way through this, together.

With their decision made, they set out once more, their footsteps echoing through the dimly lit corridors of the haunted house. And as they journeyed deeper into the unknown, they felt a sense of purpose driving them onward—a belief that they were being guided by forces beyond their understanding, toward a destination that held the key to their salvation.

As they navigated the treacherous terrain, they encountered obstacles at every turn—traps, pitfalls, and hidden dangers that tested their courage and resolve. But with each challenge they overcame, their bond grew stronger, their trust in one another unwavering in the face of adversity.

And as they pressed forward, guided by the flickering light of hope that burned within their hearts, they knew that no matter what trials lay ahead, they would face them with courage and determination, united in their quest to find their way out of the darkness and into the light of a new day.

Revelations in the Darkness

As the group forged ahead, their determination unwavering despite the trials they faced, they stumbled upon a chamber unlike any they had encountered before. The air grew heavy with anticipation as they cautiously entered, their senses on high alert for any signs of danger.

Ava: (voice trembling) What... what is this place?

The chamber was unlike any they had seen, its walls adorned with ancient symbols and cryptic markings that seemed to pulse with an otherworldly energy. As they explored further, they discovered a series of intricate carvings etched into the stone—a narrative of events long past, shrouded in mystery and intrigue.

Marcas: (voice filled with awe) It's... it's like a record of the history of this place.

Hazel: (examining the carvings closely) But what does it all mean?

As they pieced together the fragments of the story told by the carvings, a sense of unease settled over them—a realization that the secrets of the haunted house ran deeper than they had ever imagined.

Ria: (voice tinged with apprehension) There's something here... something we're not seeing.

Advik: (eyes narrowing) We need to keep searching. There has to be more to this than meets the eye.

With each passing moment, their curiosity grew, driving them deeper into the heart of the chamber in search of answers. But as they delved further into the mysteries that surrounded them, they soon found themselves confronted by a truth more terrifying than they could have ever imagined.

Dev: (voice barely above a whisper) This... this changes everything.

With their minds reeling from the revelations they had uncovered, the group stood in stunned silence, their thoughts consumed by the implications of what they had learned. And as they struggled to make sense of the truths that lay hidden in the darkness, they knew that their journey was far from over—that the answers they sought lay just beyond their reach, waiting to be discovered in the depths of the haunted house.

CHAPTER XXVIII

Echoes of the Past

As the group continued their exploration of the chamber, they stumbled upon a hidden alcove concealed behind a crumbling wall. Intrigued, they cautiously approached, their hearts pounding with anticipation as they uncovered a cache of ancient artifacts nestled within.

Hazel: (eyes widening in wonder) Look at this...

Among the artifacts lay a collection of weathered scrolls and crumbling manuscripts, their pages yellowed with age but their contents still legible to those who dared to decipher them. With trembling hands, they carefully unfurled the scrolls, revealing a trove of knowledge that spoke of a time long forgotten.

Ava: (voice filled with excitement) These... these must be records of the people who once lived here.

Ria: (examining the manuscripts closely) It's like we're peering into the past, seeing the world through their eyes.

As they pored over the ancient texts, a sense of wonder filled the air—a realization that they were not alone in their journey, but rather following in the footsteps of those who had come before them. With each new discovery, they felt a connection to the past, a bond that transcended time and space.

Marcas: (voice filled with reverence) It's as if... as if their stories are echoing through the ages, guiding us on our own journey.

Advik: (nodding) We have to keep searching. There's still so much we don't know.

With renewed determination, they delved deeper into the mysteries of the chamber, their minds ablaze with curiosity as they sought to uncover the secrets that lay hidden within. And as they pieced together the fragments of the past, they knew that their quest for truth was far from over—that the echoes of history would continue to guide them on their journey through the haunted house and beyond.

The Guardians' Legacy

As the group delved deeper into the chamber, they stumbled upon a hidden compartment tucked away in the shadows. With trembling hands, they cautiously opened it, revealing a trove of artifacts that sparkled with an otherworldly light.

Hazel: (gasping in awe) What... what are these?

Within the compartment lay a collection of ancient relics, each one pulsating with a radiant energy that seemed to defy explanation. Among them, they discovered an ornate amulet, a shimmering crystal, and a set of intricately carved stones, each one imbued with a sense of power and purpose.

Ava: (voice filled with wonder) It's like... like they're guardians of some ancient power.

Ria: (examining the artifacts closely) But what do they do? And why are they here?

As they pondered the significance of the artifacts, a sense of understanding began to dawn upon them—a realization that they were not mere trinkets, but rather keys to unlocking the mysteries of the haunted house and the secrets that lay hidden within.

Dev: (voice filled with determination) These... these must be the key to our escape. We have to use them to find a way out of here.

Advik: (nodding) He's right. We can't let these artifacts go to waste. They hold the key to our salvation.

With a sense of purpose burning bright within them, they each took hold of an artifact, their hands tingling with the power that pulsed within. And as they prepared to venture forth into the unknown, they knew that they carried with them the legacy of the guardians who had come before them—a legacy that would guide them on their journey and lead them to the truth that lay hidden at the heart of the haunted house.

CHAPTER XXIX

The Final Trial

Armed with the artifacts they had discovered, the group pressed onward, their steps guided by the pulsating energy that emanated from the relics in their grasp. As they navigated the twisting corridors and treacherous passageways of the haunted house, they felt a sense of purpose driving them forward—a determination to uncover the truth and find a way out of the darkness that had consumed them for so long.

Hazel: (voice filled with determination) We're getting closer. I can feel it.

Her words were met with nods of agreement from the others, their hearts filled with a newfound sense of hope as they drew nearer to their goal. But even as they pressed forward, they knew that their journey was far from over—that the final trial awaited them, lurking in the shadows like a specter waiting to strike.

Ria: (eyes scanning their surroundings) Be on your guard, everyone. We don't know what dangers lie ahead.

With each step they took, the air grew heavier, the darkness pressing in around them like a suffocating cloak. But despite the fear that threatened to consume them, they pressed onward, their determination unyielding in the face of adversity.

As they ventured deeper into the heart of the haunted house, they encountered obstacles at every turn—traps, illusions, and malevolent forces that sought to thwart their progress. But with each challenge they overcame, their resolve grew stronger, their bond as a group unbreakable in the face of danger.

And as they finally reached the climax of their journey, standing before the final trial that would test their courage and resolve like never before, they knew that they would face it together, united in their quest for freedom and redemption. For in the darkness of the haunted house, they had found not only the strength to survive, but the power to overcome any obstacle that stood in their way.

Darkness Descends

As the group braced themselves for the final trial, a sense of foreboding hung heavy in the air, like a dark cloud looming on the horizon. With each step they took, the tension mounted, their hearts pounding with a mixture of fear and determination.

Suddenly, without warning, tragedy struck. In the midst of the chaos, Marcas fell victim to a malevolent force, his life snuffed out in an instant. The group stood frozen in shock, their minds reeling with disbelief as they stared at the lifeless form of their friend.

Ava: (voice trembling) No... no, this can't be happening.

Ria: (struggling to hold back tears) Marcas... we have to do something.

But even as they grappled with their grief, the darkness descended upon them once more, a malevolent force that threatened to consume them all. With a sense of urgency, they knew that they had to act quickly, or risk losing everything they had fought so hard to protect.

Dev: (voice filled with determination) We can't stay here. We have to keep moving.

Advik: (nodding) He's right. We can't let Marcas's sacrifice be in vain. We have to find a way out of here, for his sake and ours.

Hazel: (wiping away tears) But... but we can't just leave him here.

With heavy hearts, they knew that they had no choice but to leave their fallen comrade behind, at least for the time being. With a final, lingering glance at Marcas's lifeless form, they turned and fled, their minds consumed with grief and their hearts heavy with sorrow.

And as they raced through the darkness, pursued by unseen forces that seemed to grow stronger with each passing moment, they knew that their journey was far from over. But with the memory of their fallen friend spurring them on, they refused to give up hope, determined to find a way out of the haunted house and into the light of day once more.

CHAPTER XXX

Into the Light

As they fled from the darkness that pursued them relentlessly, the group found themselves enveloped in a somber silence, their thoughts consumed by the memory of their fallen friend. Each step they took was heavy with the weight of grief, their hearts burdened by the loss of someone so dear to them.

Ria: (voice barely above a whisper) I can't believe he's gone...

Ava: (tears streaming down her face) He was... he was our friend.

Hazel: (voice choked with emotion) We have to... we have to keep going. For him.

Their words hung in the air, a silent tribute to the friend they had lost and the journey they had shared together. But even as they mourned his passing, they knew that they could not afford to dwell on their grief—not when their lives were still in grave danger.

Dev: (voice filled with determination) Marcas wouldn't want us to give up. We have to keep moving forward, no matter what.

Advik: (nodding) He's right. We owe it to Marcas to see this through to the end.

With a shared sense of purpose, they pressed onward, their footsteps echoing through the dimly lit corridors of the haunted house. But even as they ventured deeper into the darkness, they knew that their journey was far from over—that the trials they faced would only grow more perilous with each passing moment.

And as they continued on their quest for freedom and redemption, they carried with them the memory of their fallen friend, a beacon of light in the darkness that guided them ever forward, toward the promise of a new day and the hope of a brighter tomorrow.

The group moved through the haunted house in solemn silence, their hearts heavy with grief and their spirits weighed down by the loss of their friend. Each step they took seemed to echo with the emptiness left behind by Marcas's absence, a reminder of the void that now existed within their midst.

Ria: (voice choked with sorrow) I keep expecting him to be there, walking beside us...

Ava: (sniffling) It doesn't feel real, like... like he's still with us somehow.

Hazel: (eyes downcast) I can't believe we'll never hear his voice again, never see his smile...

Their words hung in the air, a chorus of mourning for the friend they had lost and the memories they had shared together. The weight of their sorrow seemed to press down upon them like a suffocating blanket, threatening to overwhelm them with its crushing embrace.

Dev: (voice thick with emotion) I miss him... I miss him so much.

Advik: (placing a comforting hand on Dev's shoulder) We all do, Dev. But we have to stay strong, for each other.

With a heavy heart, they continued on their journey, their eyes cast downward as they trudged through the darkness that surrounded them. But even as they mourned their loss, they knew that they could not afford to let their grief consume them—not when their lives were still in peril, and the darkness still loomed ahead.

And so, with tears in their eyes and sorrow in their hearts, they pressed onward, guided by the memory of their fallen friend and the hope of finding a way out of the haunted house and into the light of day once more.

As the group pressed forward, their resolve hardened by the trials they had faced and the memory of their fallen friend, they found themselves confronted by a final obstacle—the heart of the haunted house itself. With trepidation in their hearts and determination in their souls, they braced themselves for the ultimate confrontation.

Ria: (voice filled with determination) We can't let fear hold us back. We have to face whatever lies ahead, together.

Ava: (nodding) We've come too far to turn back now. We have to see this through to the end.

With a shared sense of purpose, they pushed open the doors that stood before them, stepping out into the blinding light of day. But their moment of triumph was short-lived, for they soon found themselves surrounded by figures cloaked in shadow, their eyes glowing with malevolence.

Hazel: (voice trembling) What... what are they?

Advik: (clenching his fists) It doesn't matter. We can't let them stop us now.

With a cry of defiance, they launched themselves into battle, their fists flying and their hearts filled with determination. With each blow they struck, they felt the darkness recede, until at last, they stood victorious over their foes.

Dev: (breathless) We did it... we actually did it.

But their victory was short-lived, for as the dust settled and the figures lay defeated at their feet, they found themselves faced with a revelation that would shake them to their core—the truth of Prisha's family, and the role they had played in the horrors that had befallen them.

Ria: (eyes wide with realization) Prisha's... she's related to the owners of this house.

Ava: (voice filled with disbelief) But... but why would they do this?

As they grappled with the enormity of what they had uncovered, they knew that they could not keep the truth hidden any longer. With heavy hearts, they made their way to Marcas's family home, where they were met by his father, Edward, and his brother, Joseph.

Edward: (voice trembling) What... what happened to my son?

Ria: (taking a deep breath) We... we lost him. But we found the truth, about Prisha's family and the haunted house.

Joseph: (eyes wide with shock) You mean... you mean they were behind it all?

As they recounted their journey and the trials they had faced, they saw the pain and sorrow reflected in Edward and Joseph's eyes, and knew that their world would never be the same again. But even as they mourned the loss of their friend and the innocence they had lost along the way, they knew that their journey was far from over.

For as they stood together, united in their grief and their determination to uncover the truth, they felt a sense of foreboding wash over them—a whisper of darkness that lingered on the edge of their consciousness, threatening to pull them back into the depths of the haunted house once more.

And as they looked to the horizon, they knew that their journey was only just beginning—that the darkness they had faced was but a prelude to the horrors that awaited them in the days to come. And with a heavy heart and a steely resolve, they braced themselves for the challenges that lay ahead, knowing that their adventure was far from over.

The End... Or is it?..